MAX & MOLLY'S SUMMER

Written and Illustrated

by

Ann Garrison Greenleaf

DERRYDALE BOOKS
New York • Avenel, New Jersey

FOR AARON

This 1993 edition is published by Derrydale Books,
distributed by Outlet Book Company, Inc., a Random House Company,
40 Engelhard Avenue, Avenel, New Jersey 07001,
by arrangement with the author.

Random House
New York • Toronto • London • Sydney • Auckland

Printed and bound in the United States of America

ISBN 0-517-09154-2

10 9 8 7 6 5 4 3 2 1

One splash and then another,

And the lazy days

drift by;

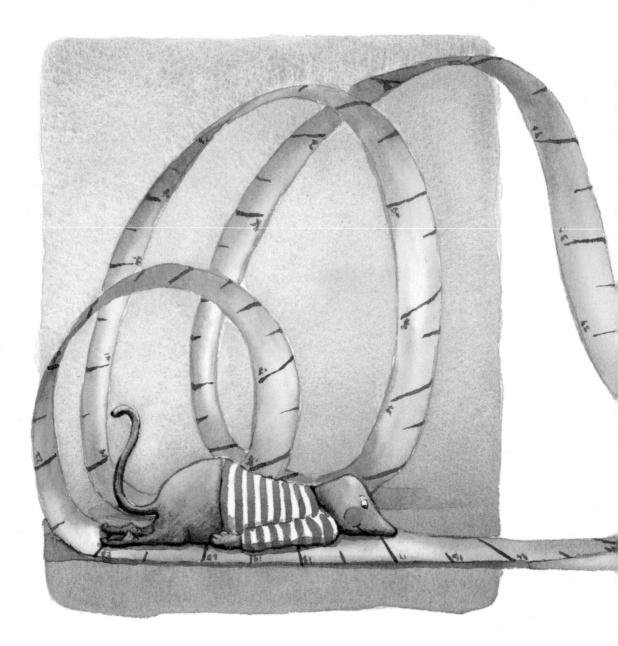

One inch

and then another,

And the corn

is six feet high.

One hop

and then another,

And the race

ends in a tie;

One spark

and then another,

And bright colors

light the sky.

One tug

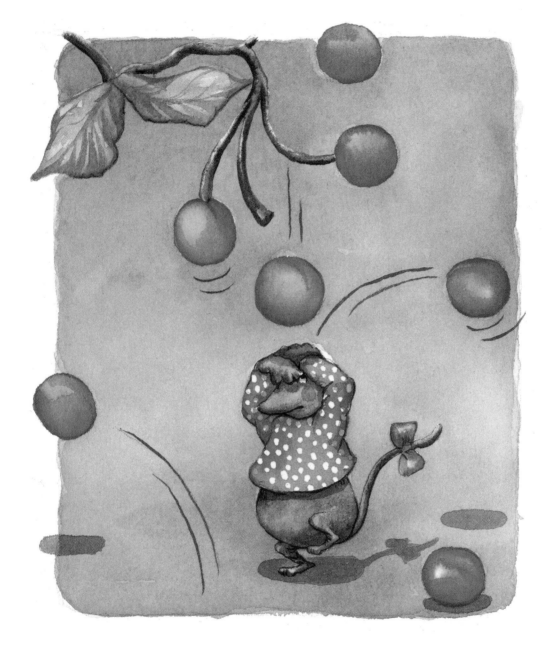

and then another,

And it's time

to pick and hull;

One jar

and then another,

And the pantry shelves

are full.

One note

and then another,

And the fiddlers

strike a tune;

One star

and then another,

And the evening ends too soon.